Mrs. McClosky's Monkeys

BY ELVIRA WOODRUFF

ILLUSTRATED BY
JILL KASTNER

SCHOLASTIC
HARDCOVER

SCHOLASTIC INC. / New York

Library of Congress Cataloging-in-Publication Data

Woodruff, Elvira.
Mrs. McClosky's monkeys.
Summary: When Mrs. McClosky's three rambunctious boys wake up one day and find they have
turned into monkeys, Mrs. McClosky takes them to live at the zoo where they are a big hit.
[1. Monkeys—Fiction. 2. Behavior—Fiction. 3. Humorous stories]
I. Kastner, Jill, ill. II. Title.
PZ7.W8606Mr 1991   [E]   90-8774

ISBN 0-590-41233-7

12 11 10 9 8 7 6 5 4 3 2 1   1 2 3 4 5 6/9

Printed in the U.S.A.   36

First Scholastic printing, April 1991
Designed by Anna DiVito

For Franny and J.P.
who know all about monkeys
—E.W.

For the monkeys of my childhood:
Mark, Joelle, and Doug
and for our newest addition, Holly
—J.K.

Mrs. McClosky had three boys, Martin, Michael, and Max.

It was the first day of their summer vacation.

Martin was so happy that he jumped on his bed until
the springs popped out!

Michael was so happy that he leapt from the couch
to the rocking chair and knocked over the lamp!

And Max was so happy that he climbed on top of the
refrigerator and ate all of the jelly beans!

The only one who was not happy was Mrs. McClosky.
"Oh, these boys!" she wailed. "No, they aren't boys,
they're monkeys! That's what I have. Three monkeys!"

That night, while the three McClosky brothers slept,
a strange thing happened:

Martin began to get furry all over!

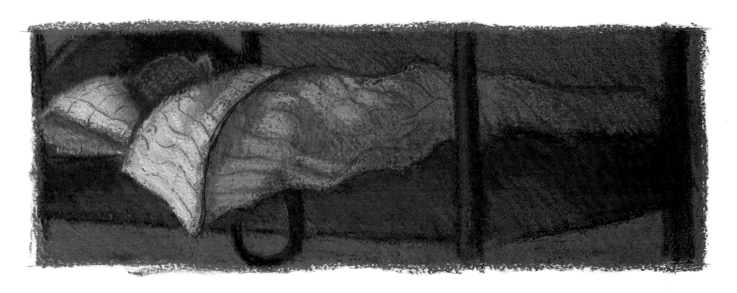

Michael began to grow a long tail!

And Max sprouted little monkey ears as he lay
dreaming of banana splits!

When her boys came down to breakfast the next morning, Mrs. McClosky groaned to her husband, "Oh, no, now they're even beginning to look like monkeys!"

As the summer went on, things grew worse. Mrs. McClosky spent all her time trying to get her boys to behave. But the McClosky brothers only wanted to behave like monkeys.

"Martin, stop swinging from that tree!" she called.

"Michael, come down from that roof!" she hollered.

"And Max, pick up all these banana peels!"
Mrs. McClosky was beside herself.
What was she going to do?

One day Mrs. McClosky took her boys to visit the zoo. They ran straight for the monkey house! And they began to act worse than ever!

A crowd gathered around to watch.

"Fine-looking monkeys you have there!" the zookeeper said to Mrs. McClosky. "We could use some new monkeys. How about letting them live here at the zoo for a while?" he asked.

Mrs. McClosky wasn't so sure. But the three little McCloskys thought this was a wonderful idea! They jumped up and down and pleaded until their mother agreed to let them stay.

"Remember to brush your teeth and wash behind your ears," she called sadly as she left the zoo.

"Oh, yes! We will! We will!" The three little McCloskys grinned as they waved good-bye.

It was great fun living at the zoo! There were bars to swing on, and tunnels to crawl through, and best of all were the crowds that came to cheer and throw peanuts!

Soon, everyone was coming to the zoo to see them! The zookeeper even put up a special big sign.

Martin, Michael, and Max
spent hours doing marvelous
monkey tricks!

Martin liked to stick
his tail between the bars
and tease the visitors.

Michael would wait
and ambush the hippos
with peanut shells as they
came out of the water!

And Max would swing
upside down from his toes
while eating a banana!

But before too long the McClosky monkeys became
bored with life at the zoo. Looking at all the people made
them homesick. They missed their mother and father and
they missed their friends.

Soon they stopped doing monkey tricks altogether.
They began to just sit in their cage and daydream about
going home and being free again.

The zookeeper had to take down the big sign, for the McClosky monkeys just weren't doing anything marvelous at all! People stopped coming to see them.

Finally, the zookeeper had to call Mrs. McClosky.

"I'm sorry, but you'll have to come and get your monkeys," he told her. "They've become the most boring monkeys we've ever had. Why, they don't even look like monkeys anymore." He frowned.

But this was just fine with Mrs. McClosky. She had missed her three little McCloskys, and so she hurried to the zoo to pick them up.

And sure enough, by the time Mrs. McClosky arrived at the zoo, there stood Martin, Michael, and Max, three very fine-looking McClosky boys. And they spent the rest of the summer looking just that way.

Well, almost!